SOLSTICE

A Mystery of the Season

SOLSTICE

A Mystery of the Season

BY

JAN ADKINS

WoodenBoat Books, Brooklin, Maine

Copyright 2004 by Jan Adkins

Published by WoodenBoat Publications Inc
Naskeag Road, PO Box 78
Brooklin, Maine 04616 USA
www.woodenboat.com

ISBN: 0-937822-81-7

Originally published by Houghton Mifflin Co, 1978

Written and illustrated by Jan Adkins

Printed in Canada by Friesens

This book is dedicated
to my sister
J U D Y
good mother, wife, friend, loony.
She is kind and generous and patient
with her brother. She leads me
beside the still waters.

SOLSTICE

A Mystery of the Season

It was a warm spell in a cold season. Spruces that had held themselves stiff and prickly against other late Decembers relaxed, and their fragrance spread across the water. The boy could smell their sharp spice in the breeze from the shore. He could smell the uncovering flats, the woodsmoke from chimneys in the spruces, the sea itself: that thin blade of smell that moved through everything.

It was warm, but only for December, so he tried again to nest his neck into his shoulders and find the deepest parts of his jacket pockets. He looked aft to his father, who showed the boy part of a smile and closed it again, looking off ahead to the islands.

The boy's eyes stayed on his father's face, trying to read some loosening, some sign. He saw that the sadness was still deep in his father's face, but was it lighter or heavier over his eyes? Did the cold bay water comfort him or excite him? The boy could not tell. The sadness had been there too long. Why were they here, a summer place in the low place of winter? The drone of the outboard engine separated the boy and his father: like eggs in a carton of noise, they were two still shapes.

The water ahead, toward the islands, was still, with the slight, linear pattern of split slate. Nearer the boat, though, the water began a dizzy rush that blurred past them, ripping itself around the boat and scrolling out behind. Aft, it was still again.

They were alone on the bay. They had been alone for two days, driving up from Boston to Bath and then out the long finger of land to Five Islands. It was almost Christmas, five days short. Why were they here?

The boy, Charlie, had been alone before the trip: he had put himself into another kind of egg carton because he couldn't listen to the shouting and the silences without cring-ing so hard his wrists and elbows hurt. He had backed away, the soft part of him, and left only a blank front in the angry house. They saw him every day, spoke to him, even paid special attention to him, guilty that their anger cut him so deeply. But they were too hurt, themselves, to know that he was really gone.

Yet Charlie felt guilt. Why couldn't he help? There were only three people in his family, and one of them hadn't helped the other two; he had only retreated; embarrassed, confused, and frightened by the knives in their talk, the flashing edges of their accusations. Yes, his father was wrong; Charlie had seen stubborness and depression swell into his father's face when they argued, heard the fragile strain in his voice. His mother was wrong, too; it was easy to belittle a man who hated himself, but she could only make her defense by hurting him. She didn't hear the pleading in his shouts or the begging to follow when he stalked from the room. Charlie did. He knew, and he should have done something. At least he should have tried.

Now father and son played a game. Al Ives sat aft, steering the outboard motor, making a long graph behind them that charted some monotonous, barely noticeable rise and fall of a minor commodity. He glanced down from the horizon and met Charlie's eyes; he winked at him and tried a smile that didn't manage to be funny or comfortable. The game was simple but very difficult to play well: they played at being normal. I don't know and You don't know and We don't know anything is wrong. We're doing normal things. We're boating on the bay in midwinter for good reason. Everyone leaves their homes seven days before Christmas and wrestles a boat into the water and makes for a deserted summer island. Nothing is wrong.

December twenty-first. The shortest day of the year. The sun was low already. It had taken a long time, horsing the old wooden garvey out of the boatshed—colder inside than outside, hoarding the damp chill of the sea night—and

launching it from its night-cold steel trailer. His father had lost his summer water confidence to the cold. He avoided the touch of a wave as if it were fire, skipping back delicately as the swell of the bay lapped against the ramp and boarding the open boat with exaggerated caution. Starting the fifteen-horse motor had taken fifty swearing, dead-coughing, back-twisting pulls and a terrible effort of his father's weak control. They were both tired when they pushed off, both tense, and the day was dimming into flat shadows and pale yellow light.

They rounded Bar Island and started up the passage. The wind hauled around behind them and their speed matched it, suspending them in a moving calm. Charlie felt warmer.

Beyond the two dozen wind-whittled spruces of little Bar Island was the long wooded outline of Loud's Island, a two-mile slab of granite and spruce needles rising out of Muscongus Bay. The cabin on it had been in his father's family for fifty years, used as a summer place. Charlie thought it had probably been used too much; it had electricity and running water and an old Dodge pickup truck that sat the winter up on blocks in a shed. Charlie would have preferred Loud's rough, as wild as the weed, rock, and flotsam shore. It was life on an island that was magic to him, away and queer, like living in another time—the lights, the toilets, only reminded him that he would go back to the city . . . and the arguments, and the silent dinners, and three people carving lines of territory in the same house.

In the winters he dreamed of the island . . . but not like this, braced in the cold wind off the winter Atlantic, stiff with frost even in a warm spell.

The island didn't charm his mother. The broken shore didn't appeal to her, the distanced island life wasn't magic, the convenience of electricity and plumbing didn't take the edge off her dislike for the place. To her it was just a slum on vacation. Charlie tried to understand; she had been one of twelve children in a family where clean tables and clean floors were daily labor, where all twelve (at least the five sisters) determined to have a neat, quiet, respectable house. His father called it "lace curtain gentility, first generation." She avoided talking about the island, evaded their trips to it. Charlie looked aft along the lengthening water path the boat made, following it to shore and beyond, and he saw his mother at the kitchen table in Boston, drinking coffee and watching the birdfeeder. Was she thinking about them? He didn't think so.

His father loved the island. He seemed young when he was on it, as young as Charlie. He left his city-self on a peg in the boatshed. After his black moods had started, the island was the only place where he relinquished his anger and stopped being a victim. His overrevving mind slowed; sometimes he sat looking at the water for hours. On the island he seemed to be smelling things, always: *Charlie, smell the resin in the air, smell the rookery, take a whiff of that . . . they must be haying on the mainland . . .*

The Whaler sliced around a torn tree trunk, washed down the Damariscotta River from who knows how far upstream to find a home in the sea. He looked to his father to see if his nostrils flared at the rank smell of oak, but couldn't tell.

It was too early to know what his father's mood was. The boat was too cold and difficult to let him relax, yet. Maybe on the island he would uncoil, and the lines pushing down above his eyes would smooth. Maybe he could do familiar, simple things, uncomplicated, old things. Maybe he would do boy things and unsnarl the roots of confusion that his city life fed, roots that twisted inside his head until his forehead knotted in lines of worry. Charlie knew, somehow, that if his father had stayed this Christmas in the grip of his city sadness he would burn out black and hollow like a spent flare. So Charlie had gone with him, abandoning his mother and his home and everything just before

Christmas. Christmas was supposed to be so . . . what was it? Holy? Special? Powerful? So why was Christmas so hard? Charlie asked himself. It was the first time he had ever questioned Christmas; he didn't know that his question was asked by everyone after a certain carelessness of childhood wore away. He stared at the water boiling past the boat, saddened by the question.

But why was Christmas hard? Wasn't it supposed to be the happiest time of the year? He thought back to other Christmases, remembering them now in a different light, seeing the hard lines around smiling mouths, hearing the pleasant phrases spoken harshly. His impressions of the happy holiday had been sugarcoated. He pried up the boards of memory, and recalled cross faces and crying during the dinners and the carol sings.

But he was young enough to shut the memories away for now, knowing as he sat inside the shell of motor noise that the memories were sprung now, like planks in a wooden boat, and the truth would seep in like cold water.

What kind of Christmas dinner would they have on the island? They had waited too long on the drive up to stop for food at a big market. A lot of the little stores were Closed for the Season, See You Next Summer. His father had bought some rum, some eggs from a chicken lady near the landing, some dairy-store milk and bread and orange juice. Egg sandwiches, corned beef sandwiches—Christmas dinner. Charlie looked in the bag beside him. Potato chips.

The motor died.

"Stupid sonofabitch." Al Ives stood and kicked the motor. "You bitch," he said kicking it harder. He yanked the starter.

"Is it out of gas?" Charlie asked.

"How far have we gone? Thirty miles? Forty miles? Use some sense, you idiot. We've gone three miles. If that. With a full tank of gas. Are we out of gas!"

Charlie felt his father's anger shift from the motor to him. His father's tone was so sharp and ragged and ironic that although Charlie knew his father didn't really mean it for him, he felt cut and torn, as if the words were a barbed-wire fence ripping past. His father's voice lashed at him again, but Charlie knew it was only his voice, that the man didn't want to.

"So we're not out of gas, no. Do you have any other brilliant suggestions or do you want to shut up and let me solve the problem?" Charlie tried not to hear his sneering, belittling words; he tried to read the words in his eyes that said, Help me, Charlie, I don't want to say this, get me out of this whirl-pool, I'm drowning in anger and sadness. . . .

But Charlie was too hurt to help, and the words in Al's eyes still had no sound, so they sep-arated in a silence that was made more desperate by the wheezing of the failed motor.

The wind and the tide took them away. They drifted up the passage and away from Loud's Island as the light drained out through a hole in the sunset. The islands farther north be-came indistinct, and in the thickening night-gloom the motor's refusal seemed louder, over and over, until Al's hand was blistered from the starter cord and he stopped.

"I thought we were supposed to have oars," Charlie said. "I thought it was the law." He re-membered oars in the corner of the boatshed and he was frightened enough to risk the words. "We could swim for it. It's not a quarter-mile. I can swim that easy. I can swim half—"

"Damn it! Will you be quiet? You wouldn't get a hundred yards in this water before the cold stopped you. You wouldn't be able to feel your arms or cup your hands in twenty yards. Your feet and legs wouldn't work after . . . no, look, I'll give the old engine a rest and then it will work just fine . . . just fine." He had frightened himself. What could he do about the motor? It didn't feel right. There was no life in it when he spun it. This place, this water, was not his friend, now. Where were they going?

They might fetch up on Marsh Island, across from Loud's, if they drifted that far. The image of the boat drifting out into the bay, being lifted by big swells, thrown onto a ledge, overturned, his son slipping away helpless . . . Al Ives wanted to howl like a dog and confess every bad thing he had ever done, to humble himself before all the gods, to admit his smallness and weakness, if only they could get home safely. Oh, please. Still, the motor would not start.

If the water was not their friend, the tide was, and the cold wind. As Al fussed with the dead motor and Charlie snuggled himself into the lee of the steering console, they drifted upchannel more quickly than they noticed. When only a gray skim of light was left they were in the gut between the islands, where a backloop of the wind blew them east, toward Marsh.

They drifted past a headland where a small cove opened up and there, not a hundred feet away, a lantern swung from a scrub tree, lighting a footpath that led up steeply from the pebbled beach.

"Charlie! Look at that! There's someone on the island. They must be expecting someone." The light danced and swayed until they realized that the current was taking them past the cove.

"Paddle, Charlie! With your hands, with anything. Use that seat cushion. I'll use . . ." He looked around and tore the cover off the cooler, leaning over the port side and pushing the water back furiously. Fury didn't work; the squarish Whaler spun more than moved. They had to work together, listening to the rhythm, feeling the boat, correcting with every stroke. A ledge of rock reached out toward them. If they could just get inside it before the tide swept them upchannel . . . they quickened their splashing and synchronized it as much as desperation would allow.

Rock grated against the white plywood with a rough boom. Al leaped out and embraced the rock, half-in and half-out of the stinging water, not noticing its bite. "The painter, Charlie, get me the painter before I lose it."

Charlie dropped the cushion and clambered forward to find the bow line in the deep shadows. He leaped with it onto the rock, but the rock felt liquid. Unreal.

His father came up out of the water. Charlie reached a steadying hand to him, and Al kept holding on to it after they were both standing, grinning. Viewed from safety, the disaster had become an adventure. Al put his arm around the boy, pulling him into him against the wind. They were both soaked to the waist. "Come on, Charlie, let's drag this thing over into the cove and see what kind of help we can get."

The garvey was up on the shingle with a second line bent to the painter and hitched to a tree. Charlie and his father started up the path, then hesi-tated. "I think the lantern might be for us." Charlie said. Al looked at him and shrugged, then nodded. Charlie went back for the lantern and they entered the dense forest.

They threaded through a tunnel of thick spruces, over plaited roots that fingered out beneath them, skirting huge, pale boulders. The kerosene lantern cast shadows that reeled and shook as darkness closed in behind them. The wind made noises in the spruce tips above them while leaves rustled at their ankles. All sense of direc-tion and distance, even time, faltered after the first fifty yards. They did not know where they were.

The forest opened suddenly again, to the water and the sky.

The last thin light, across the channel and over Loud's, shaded from a magically deep blue, through an unearthly purple, to a star-pricked indigo. The sky was framed by ragged branches and anchored to a tiny cabin snugly fitted with just-so door and just-so windows, shingled precisely and recently. One half of the little camp reached out over the tidal ledge twenty feet below. The other half was moored to a red brick chimney that gestured with curls of sweet-scented balsam smoke. The cabin glowed from within like a toy train depot.

The two of them stood amazed, forgetting the cold, forgetting for a moment their own world and believing suddenly in faeries, or magic.

A voice came from behind them like a thunderclap.

"Thought you was gonna miss the cove. Whole damn thing."

"Aa!" Al shouted involuntarily and fell back.

A man walked between them and continued down the path to the porch of the cabin. Without looking back he said, "Bring a stick o' this wood when you come in. You come along, now, and get warm."

Charlie, his heart hammering, took his father's hand.

They walked down to a clean-swept porch and ducked under the eaves to stand at the door, where they called out, "May we come in?"

"You come right in." The

door opened. "Over here by the stove, right up beside it there."

"Thank you. Oh, yes, this heat feels . . ." Al and Charlie spread their hands to the black iron of the stove and hunched their shoulders toward it. "Feels absolutely good. You are a lifesaver. I feel really stupid. I'm Alban Ives, from Boston. And my boy Charlie. From Boston. You see, we were going over to Loud's Island for a few days and our motor . . ."

"No oars," the old man said as he helped them out of their coats. "You trust them en-gines, don't ya? Not me. Y' can't trust 'em, not the best one ever put together. And you can't trust the wind either, come down to that. Y' can trust y'self. Maybe. Oars is simple enough not to

have the brains to go wrong on ya. Here. Wet things off and get these blankets 'round ya. Sit right there on the bed. 'Nother blanket for y'feet. Dry these things out."

He was a small man attached to a huge pair of hands, tan and yellow with groves of white hair on the backs up to the knuckles. His hands moved constantly, picking up, putting down, arranging, stirring a pot on the wide stove, and flexing restlessly when they hung at his sides. His face hid behind a gray-and-white beard that wasn't successful in hiding the eyes, pale bluish-gray eyes that were quick and straight to you. The crinkles around them could have come from squinting at the sun or from laughing

or from both. His hair was white and full and looked as if he'd cut it himself with kitchen shears.

Charlie figured he lived by himself because he talked to himself, discussing each thing he did in slight murmurs. "Oh, yes, get somethin' hot into them storm orphans. Land of mercy. Stir this soup so she don't burn, just so, just so."

It was the smell of the pot on the stove that made the boy and father remember themselves: a sweet, rich aroma of seafood and spices, onions and celery leaves. Suddenly they were terribly hungry, chilled to the bone, and so tired that bending to untie their shoes seemed like climbing a ten-foot wall.

Their socks and underwear hung on mitten warming rods

that swung out from the stove. Their pants and shirts and sweaters hung close around the stove on lengths of cord, steaming slightly. Their leather shoes stood formally at attention at a respectful distance. Father and son sat wrapped in blankets on the bed while the old man kneeled before them, swaddling their feet in another blanket.

"I'm so grateful"—Charlie's father was awkward and sincere—"a day like this, finding you, being cared for. We don't deserve it."

The old man leaned back with his hands on his knees and shook his head, smiling. His eyes were filmed over with tears. "No such a thing. Deserve more'n you got here, that's for sure." He sniffled. "Stove fumes. Get at ya. Charlie, huh?" He swatted the boy's knee playfully.

"Vern Filson," he said, "that's me. And you don't know it, but you come at the right time. You know when you've come? No. Course you don't. Not many do. Big day. Little one, really." He was back at the stove wiping his fume-stung eyes with a towel, stirring the pot. He reached down to a woodbox, then lifted a back disc from the stovetop with an iron-pronged handle to drop short splits of wood into the firebox. A tongue of flame licked up out of the hole, but the old man closed it again and turned quickly.

"Christmas Eve! Ha! Didn't know that, did ya?"

Al brought his watch up out of the blankets. Twelve twenty-one. Digital accuracy. "Well, it's almost Christmas Eve, but we'd be rushing it."

"One of them calendar watches, in't it? Oh, I know what day it is, hell yes. It's not the day I got wrong. It's the whole damned idea they got wrong! Yessuh. It's Christmas Eve, okay.

"Here, you need something to warm you from inside. Just a little something cause supper's later on. I'm thinking the boys will come. Yuh, I think they'll make it in time. Ladle out two. Two mugs, 'long with two spoons, there ya go." He put them into their still unsteady hands. He poured two jelly glasses full of brown liquids from separate jugs and put one beside the boy.

Al started again. "How can we thank y—"

"No, no, I'm thankin' you. You just don't know what a lot of good you're doin' me, comin' round here this day. Folks need folks, that's how she works. Here, Al, you drink this." He gave him the clearer, more golden drink and winked. "Plenty of warm in that."

Al brought the glass to his lips. The breath of the dark rum came into his nose on sugary curving blades and it slid fire across his tongue and down his throat and into his furnace. He closed his eyes and shook his head, but the old man was up and on the move, putting on a brown canvas hunting coat and wrapping a muffler around his neck.

"Christmas Eve," he said more to himself than to them. "Then I got work to do, don't

I?" With some fussing he lit and adjusted a lantern, then went out a door on the other side of the stove; the light showed a lean-to addition. He closed the door behind him, and soon there came the sounds of bumping and scraping and occasional tapping, along with other mysterious but domestic noises.

Al drank the fine rum and thought about how Charlie's mother had looked under the thatch of a beach bar drinking dark rum, wearing a swimsuit and one of his blue shirts unbuttoned and tied around her waist. They'd been on a vacation in the Exumas, years ago. Her name for him on that trip and for months after was "Captain Rum," or just "Captain." He was about to come back to

how he felt about her now, but he stayed with the rum and the image and kept his eyes closed.

Charlie drank his sweet cider and then held the mug of chowder in both hands, letting it warm them. He sipped at it. Potatoes and fish and milk and yellow butter spots and bits of soft onion. His eyes traveled around the cabin, as hungry for the place as for the chowder. This is the way their place on Loud's Island should be.

Charlie loved Muscongus and Penobscot Bays and their archipelagoes. He wished he could live on them all year. All his life. He did not know why they moved him; it was a mystery and he was young enough to live comfortably with mysteries. This cabin, though, had some of that mystery. In the way it appeared, almost magically, and in the way the old man was so much a part of it. And the way the place itself belonged here, almost grew out of the bay and the rocks and the spruces. The cabin was small and tight, like a boat's cabin, but square and unvarnished and homey. The wallboards still showed the parallel scour of the saws that had cut them from their logs. The beams and the posts that held them up still held the axe marks of their squaring. Tools and line and clothes hung from pegs, out of the way. A broom and dustpan hung on one side of the door, coats on the other, boots under, hats over. Things were obvious; the house worked. The dishwater drained out of the sink through a scupper in the side of the house, which was tacked around with gray lead, and dropped to the cove below. The onions and potatoes in his chowder, his delicious chowder, had shared the nets above the sink with nuts, cabbages, apples, sprigs of herbs, and a braided rope of garlic. Hanging from rafters nearby were carved wooden spoons; some small enough for one pumpkin seed, some large enough to lift a whole Maine russet potato. The green curtains at the kitchen window were old, mended. Nothing was hidden here. No drawers or cupboards, not even any paint to hide the grain of wood. A few closed sea chests, a few hanging sailbags, but bulky with folded things under their smooth facades. The clutter was as organized as a forest; it had its own order. A current of life flowed through this place, placing the pegs, organizing the two straightbacked chairs, the stool, the little table.

The lord of the cabin was the stove. It occupied a tenth of the floorspace, heated and cooked, and added the only note of decoration with its ornate scrolls of cast iron, its nickeled, vine-leafed shelf fronts, its porcelain knobs, and the white porcelain oven-door shield bearing its name: *CHARM CRAWFORD ROYAL.*

Even the pronged handle that lifted the cooktop plates had character: below the spring-wound handle bloomed a grotesque face that stuck out its tongue and spread its jowels to grasp the square inset holes in the discs. And around this king a court made its obeisance: woodboxes filled with bucksaw, axe, splitting maul, hatchet, and wedge; gray pots, black skillets, and steel utensils hung above. The wet clothes hanging above became a tapestry and added a majestic steamy mist to the scene.

Charlie finished his chowder and wondered what his father was thinking about as he held the jelly glass cupped in his hands beneath his closed eyes. He wondered when supper would be. Didn't care. Had no idea what time it was now. Realized that his eyes were closed. He leaned back, felt himself lifted up and placed on the bed with the blankets wrapping him. Later he felt his father lie beside him and put his arm over him: For the first time in many years he slept protected by his father's strong arm. Wondering about the thumping, tapping, bumping from the lean-to, he snuggled into his father and, soothed by the wash, wash of the lapping waves, slept.

He dreamed of the stove and its court, about warmth and the bay, and after that he slipped dreamless into darkness and forgetfulness of everything.

Charlie woke. On the stove the iron lidlifter's face grinned warmly and foolishly as it held itself against the hot black surface. Charlie smiled back at it.

The windows were still black; it was still early in the evening.

He could hear the old man moving about in the woodshop. His father was still asleep, with a face as peaceful as a farm dog's. When the shop door opened, a cool puff of cut-lumber fragrance mingled with the darker smell of the stove. The old man, murmuring to himself so quietly that Charlie couldn't understand, closed the door behind him. He was covered with woodshavings, dropping a few as he bustled over to the stove and collected Charlie's things. He picked them off the mitten dryers with his big, clumsy looking hands, laying them neatly over one arm, and put them down beside Charlie. He smiled at Charlie and shook his head impatiently. Hurry up!

Charlie pulled on his dry pants and was buttoning his shirt. The old man looked hes-

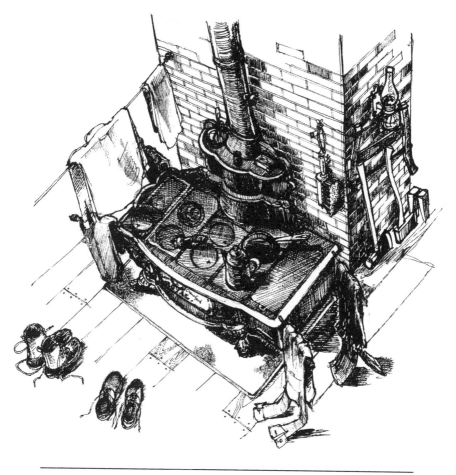

itantly at the socks, then picked them up and started tucking the cuff into neat folds; he lifted Charlie's foot and slipped one on. As he patted away the wrinkles on each foot he finally said, "Boys. Used to put my boys' socks on, come morning. When they was younger, you know." His voice was soft and throaty, talking low so as not to wake Charlie's father. The old man rose, using his hands on his knees to straighten up, and jerked his head: Come along. He picked up a pair of rubber boots from beside the door and folded the tops down as he placed them in front of Charlie. Charlie clumped after him to the shop door but the old man spun around, looking at him closely.

"Nip in the air, out there." he said, taking off his buff canvas coat and pulling it on around Charlie. He folded the corduroy collar up and buttoned it. It felt comforting to Charlie; no one had dressed him since he was five. The old man was still wearing several layers of sweaters and shirts.

The shop was cold but not unpleasant, a long, narrow space lit by three lanterns. The dusty texture of the place made it seem warmer than it was. There were stacks of rough-cut lumber under the long workbench that made up one wall; fine sawdust and spirals of woodshavings covered the floor; a dozen planks of wood leaned against the wall at the far end, shouldering each other conversationally. A metal galaxy of tools hung against the wall over the workbench. Saws and pencil-marked patterns for curving forms hung against the wall across from the bench, along with a stuffed deer head with remarkable glass eyes.

"What are you making?" Charlie asked.

The old man winked. "Later," he said, "Right now's time for *you* to make something. It's the time of year for it."

"Well, Christmas is four days away—" He stopped: the old man was shaking his head.

"Nope, it ain't. Tonight's the night, boy. Hasn't anyone ever told you about where she sits in the year? In the scheme of things? Does your father wear boots down there in Boston, Massachusetts, does he?"

"Boots? Yes, sir, black rubber ones for walking in the marsh and leather ones for walking in the woods, and cowboy boots for kind of dressing like a cowboy. But in Boston. You know."

"Good, real good. So we got it right here." He held up a wooden Y with a short leg off one side in the middle. "She's a bootjack." Charlie shook his head. "You never see one? If you wasn't such a smart boy I'd think you was a dumb one." The grin and the hundred echoes of grin lines around it took the sting out of that. "You're going to make a dandy, better'n this one any day."

"I'm not very good at making things. I don't do models or anything and we don't have shop class in our school. I'm just not good with my hands, sir."

He put the bootjack down at that, amazed. "Can you do this?" he asked, crooking his index finger up and down, waving a tiny bye-bye.

When Charlie did the same, the old man beamed, then turned and nodded to the stuffed deer head, then to Charlie. "Why, hell, you'll do fine. That's real good man-u-al dex-ter-i-ty, as they say. Do just fine, and we start right here with this here nice piece of oak. Look't that, ain't that a fine piece?"

So Charlie made a bootjack. The old man had the kind of patience that amounts to respect. He demonstrated, pointed out limits, encouraged questions, and in an unhurried way kept the pace up. They looked at the grain in the oak piece ("Real nice, grain like that, talks to you every day you

see it") and scribed a pattern. The boy learned how to hold a saw and how to address the wood and how to stroke smoothly, consistently. Vern Filson showed him the difference between saws: rip for going with the grain and crosscut for just what it sounds like. A thin-bladed jigsaw to cut out the crotch of the Y, and a stiff backsaw to make two parallel cuts on one face that would be sides for the slot that took the leg. Charlie learned to set the plane and to handle it as he smoothed the oak, held to the workbench with its vise, till the grain really did begin to speak and the piece was sleeker than sandpaper could ever have made it. ("Sandpaper. Sandpaper, my stars, that's worthless stuff to a real woodworker.") He used a chisel to take out the oak between the backsaw cuts, then smoothed the bottom of the mortise ("That's what she's called, a mortise, and right there you got the beginning of real woodwork") with an open-edged mortise plane.

"I got somewhere here a real fine little stick of ebony and I don't even know why I got it, so let's use it for the leg, Charlie." They planed it just so, Charlie overplaning the first till it was too thin for the slot. He felt bad until Vern told him to "let off scowlin' at y'self so, let's get this next one just spang on. You betcha." They did. And they tapped it in over foul-smelling glue, then tacked a little band of leather, rough side out,

around the crotch of the Y to grip the heels of the boots. Charlie had never done anything so quickly, or anything so useful, he thought. A bootjack.

While they worked, Vern told him about Christmas.

"Took me a while to figure it out. But it you figure at something long enough, and if you talk about it and listen so as to frame it up in your mind, you can figure it all out.

"Goes like this. Nothin' happens for no reason. No, sir. Got to be a reason for things, for everything. Look here, why do we have these funny shapes on these saw handles? There's a reason. I don't know what it is, but I know there is one. So look here, I says to myself, how about Christmas? Comes right in the middle of the damn winter when the main event happened over there in a place where the difference between winter and summer don't amount to much anyway, and how do we know when the big day was, I ask you? Don't know for sure at all. Fellah over at Marsh Island, teacher down at some college, told me the calendar's been all mushed over by every other emperor and king for three thousand years. That's a mighty long fishline to pin her down to one single day, now, ain't it? You bet. You're no dummy, Charlie.

"I was a lobsterman. Out there tendin' pots, sailing between strings of pots . . . "

"Do many lobstermen use sailboats now?"

The old man looked at him for a moment and Charlie was afraid he had interrupted rudely, but Vern smiled—another kind of smile, sweet with the sad set of lines cut into his face. "No, Charlie, they don't.

"Well, you've got a lot of time out there on the bay to think. And this other thought comes to me—there ain't no coincidences. Oh, I know there are, and all, but you want to be careful chalking everything up to coincidence. Now, just keep that in mind for a minute and ask yourself this: What's the saddest season of the year?"

"Fall." Charlie answered, unhesitatingly.

"Fall? Why's that?"

"School starts again."

"Now, Charlie, that's not what I was thinking. No, I was thinking winter, you see, because everything dies away. The warmth goes away from us. Weather turns against us. The garden we live in—just like the first two folks lived in a garden—we get chased out of it. We're scared into thick clothes—look at us two, right now—and chased into our houses. We worry 'bout whether we've put enough by. Have we made the house strong enough? Will we last through it or will we dry out and fade away like the squash vines and the last bean plants in the garden? It's like the earth was our mother, you see, and we don't know why she went away. What'd we do? The days get shorter, colder, and you begin, maybe, to lose hope.

"Hope's all we got, Charlie.

"But the earth spins 'round herself, and the earth swings 'round the sun, of course, and she swings around at a tilt like a lady could wear a hat if she was as beautiful as this lady Earth of ours. And the tilt, you know, makes the difference in the days. When the tilt is away from old father sun, the sunlight comes slantin' in shallow and the time for Penobscot Bay to be in the sun every day ain't much. Short, cold days. Long, fierce nights.

"Spinnin', Charlie, the word is spinnin.' It's a cycle, somethin' that comes round and comes round, and there comes up one day that's the shortest, one night that's the longest. It's called the Winter Solstice. Spinnin' on, it all gets better after that.

"What we got, then, is the Solstice. The deepwater of winter. The part when it's darkest. The part when you might give up hope. But there's hope right in it, because it's brighter after that, it's an earth promise. Every day takes us away from the worst. But we're soft people, and our hope is fragile stuff, and what we need most of all at this time of year is a celebration for hope.

"You listen to them carols—talking about hope. Talking about how the world in darkness lay, and wishing joy to the world. And the way I break it down, though I am not a churchgoin' person, you should excuse me, is that after the big event in the little town of Bethlehem everything is going to be better. Not right off. No, but coming along. Like the summer.

"So it's the dark time, Charlie, when we all step close to each other. Families"—he looked past the deer head to the window at the far end and paused a moment, listening for something Charlie could not hear—"families lean in and share. We all say, hell, yes, it's worth hanging on, thing's are getting better. We give presents—it's a little hope we give one another." He turned back to Charlie. "Oh, we're lucky, we are, when we can give a little hope. I'm lucky, lucky because of you. You're a good boy, Charlie. Your father is lucky."

He hesitated, then reached out and tousled Charlie's hair. His hand felt big and hard and warm.

"And now, you want to see something? Something just pure wonderful?"

"Sure." They had finished the bootjack and he had been rubbing linseed oil into the oak while Vern talked, trying to take it all in, seeing the earth spin, feeling the cold, thinking of his father and the cold. Thinking of his mother and the birdfeeder.

The old man put his arm around Charlie and walked down the bench to the window, a big window to get sunlight into the shop. He undid a turn-latch and swung the window out into the night, and they leaned out after it, and it was wonderful.

Up the passage where Charlie and his father had been blown, two boats rode on black

wind and silver moonlight, two dark boats whose sails in the brightest breath of the moon were red, whose rigging was touched with frost that sparkled. And in the bow of the lead boat, taking up its small foredeck, a spruce sapling was hung with red and green lanterns. They watched and, with the black wind's trick, suddenly heard a concertina and saw, now, the player, standing in the stern of his boat steering with one foot, playing a reedy, strange, wonderful jig. Up the passage, black and silver, with the red and green of the tree's lanterns and the green of their own starboard running lights. Then Charlie could see both running lights red and green as they came up into the wind and drifted into the old man's cove. There was the rasp of anchors going down, still the concertina music, and the wind. Their sails folded themselves down, laughter drifted up, two boats pulled away with a cadence of oars, and the frost-touched masts swayed in the moonlight.

Charlie looked up as the old man's side began quaking. He was crying; big, silent tears.

"Sir?" said Charlie, softly. He took the old man's hand.

"My boys." Vern said.

Al sat on the bed looking into the saucer of rum in the bottom of his mug. He swirled the mug and the reflection of his face warped away.

Here, sitting on this bed so far away from anything he knew, he seemed to think better. He could see through the haze of doom that had mired him.

Al heard Charlie and Vern working together in the shop. What were they up to? How easily they fit together.

How easily he fit with Charlie's mother, once. How can people who have had so much fun together come to have so much misery for each other?

It came to him as suddenly and with the same cutting penetration as the smell of the rum that he hadn't stopped loving. He had only grown more wary. He was afraid she had stopped loving him, that she saw him as another Charlie, as a duty to be borne. Charlie was growing up and Al was growing old.

He shook his head and shook it again. I'd like to see her, he thought. I'd like to pick her up in a Nash Rambler for a date. I'd like to see if I could put my arm around her in the movies. Al almost laughed to himself about that. That would shock her.

He heard Vern and Charlie opening a window and he heard a high, reedy sound almost like a song.

"MY BOYS . . . ," he said, scuttling across the main part of the cabin, rearranging things that didn't need rearranging. "Charlie, clear out that corner you're standin' in. Al . . . "

Al Ives had been putting on his dry clothes when the shop door burst open, and he stood, stooped over, one leg in his pants, one leg up.

"Hell, Al, y'gonna fall over. Put on them pants and you can help me with a table." He plunged into the shop at a short-legged trot and caused a great scraping and banging, then reappeared behind the butt ends of three planks that were trying not to be parallel, splaying and stopping against the doorframe and ramping suddenly to buck against the floor. The old man began to giggle, "I'm just awful at this," he said, laughing at his own foolishness. "I can't hurry worth a damn. Get excited, I do." He tried to get the planks straight. "Get all tangled." He was laughing even harder.

There were three rapid knocks at the door, schoolboy knock-and-run taps. "H'lo there!" the old man shouted and simply dropped the planks, missing his boots by a splinter-width. "Get on in here!"

No answer. He looked at Al and Charlie with a grin. "Better see who's knockin'," he said, and giggled again. He opened the door. Nothing. Then a scrape at the doorsill. "Good night, nurse!" he shouted and skipped back. A lobster almost two feet long dragged itself in, back arched, heavy claws held up and ready. "Look at that fellah, will you, he's gonna eat us all if we let him. Fierce, mighty fierce." He called out the door to his boys, "Grover! Tyler! Come in here and call off your watch-lobster 'fore he chews at us. I'm the only pa you got, y'know."

They came around the door, hooting with laughter, holding each other, and then they put their arms around their father and the three of them hooted together, ignoring the solemnly threatening lobster. Charlie watched it warily, wondering if lobsters bit and if their bite was poisonous. It certainly looked as though it was.

Vern kissed the boys through their beards and hugged them closer. "Where'd you get that monster?" They were both short and stocky, like the old man. Like him they carried enormous hands on strong, stocky arms. Their legs seemed small and agile, but their shoulders, even under their coats and sweaters were huge bows of muscle. It made Charlie think

of pulling lobster pots every day. Their faces were already fine-lined where their father's was deep-lined—tracery from the sun and the wind and the bay. They had knobby noses like his, and deep eyes like his, and all three had easy, open smiles (though Tyler's was a bit shyer).

"Tyler fouled a lost pot over in the Muscle Ridge about at Dix, pulled it with one of his. That right, Tyler?" Tyler bobbed his head, grateful not to have to talk, and Grover went on. "Must've been in there a season or two, eatin' eels and small stuff, but we was wonderin' how he got in the pot in the first place. Big'un. Tyler been keepin' him in his own lobster pound waitin' to spring

him on you. That right, Tyler?"
Bob and nod, eyes cast down.

Vern hugged Tyler again.
"He's sure a big'un," Vern said.
"Well, get in here and shut the
door and—"

Tyler, standing by the door,
shook his head adamantly.

"What? What are you up to?"
Vern asked.

"Pa," Grover said, arm
around him again, "We got another little surprise for you."

" 'Nother lobster out there or
a dead seal or what?"

"Picked up someone along
the way, Pa."

Vern was looking back at
Grover when she stepped into
the light of the door behind
him. She was a big girl, not at
all slim, but it was the face that
took you, the face and the

hands. The face was a quiet
place for large eyes the color of
waves when they rise up and
the sun comes through them
before they break. And she had
a sweet nose, not at all knobby,
and a small, soft mouth. It was
a face for caring. The hands
were gentle and finely boned,
less quiet than the face, for they
nervously comforted each
other.

Vern saw everyone looking
behind him and turned with a
great grin. The grin died, and
the old man's hands came up as
if he were about to return a vase
to a shelf. Bewilderment, sadness, even remnants of fear and
loss, made their troubled way
across his weathered face. She
never cast down those sea-
green eyes; her hands, done

with waiting, became still. She took one breath and said in a small, sweet voice, "Pa."

Grover started to say something, but Tyler put a hand on his shoulder.

Finally Vern clenched his hands to his chest. For the second time he was crying, but this was different. He was crying parts of himself out. Then he said very simply, very softly, in a tone of voice Charlie hadn't heard him use before, "Sarah."

She stepped in over the threshold and put her hands on his shoulders, her head against his big, sweatered chest. He folded his arms around her and Charlie could smell the green smell of the breeze through the door and a rose-soap smell from Sarah and the hot iron smell of the stove, and he could see the old man's shoulders bump as he tried to stop crying.

Grover, jolly and loud, would have no more of it. "Why, hell, come on in here, Nate," and another person came in, tall, thin, dark, and dressed in a black suit. Vern disengaged one hand and offered it to the man in the suit. They shook, solemnly at first and then with warmth. Grover and Tyler surrounded Vern and Sarah with their arms, leaving the dark stranger outside.

He turned to Charlie and Al and introduced himself. "Good evening. I am Nathaniel Feynman of Bangor, Maine. How do you do?"

"Damnation!" Vern shouted, disentangling himself from his children. "We got guests and here we are picknicking on our own! Mind your manners, wha-tinhell kind of father am I?"

"Grover Filson." Vern's first son stuck out his big hand to Al and Charlie. "Glad to meet you. Glad you're here. Nice night for it." Huge grin.

"I'm Al Ives, and this is my son, Charlie."

Tyler stepped up to them, put out his hand, cleared his throat, opened his mouth, and before all these preparations could come to fruition Grover spoke up. "This's Tyler, who don't speak much more'n a cod but he's real nice, sort of." Tyler squinched his eyes closed in annoyance, but opened them with an accepting grin and just nodded.

"Good evening. I'm Sarah Filson Feynman, and this is my husband." She cast down her eyes at this. "Mr. Nathaniel Feynman."

"Best damn tailor in Bangor," called Grover, and held out his coat to show off a black vest over his sweater. Tyler was pointing to his pants. "Sadie married this fellah," Grover continued, "and went off to Bangor. We thought we'd never see her again." Feynman looked studiously at the floor. "So Tyler and me up and took the train to Bangor, see, and wanted to get a look at what kind of place he's keepin' our sister in. Real nice place they got. Good food. Little noisy, but real nice."

Feynman had a little smile for the floor.

"Tell you something else. They're paintin' up a little

room in the back. Not for boarders."

Sarah blushed, trying not to smile, but Feynman the tailor had a proud little smile for the stove.

Vern cleared his throat. Too much in one gulp. "Hell!" he said. "How 'bout a little music and let's get to work on dinner!"

Vern's cry was the general signal for an all-out charge. Only Charlie and his father stood still in the midst of the rush, but not for long. The boys and Saran and Feynman bolted out the door after Vern, who returned with a stack of stove-wood laid to his chin while the boys swung in with canvas bags. Sarah strode in to the sink, carrying a long wrapped parcel;

Feynman brought in flat parcels and a small coffin-shaped case. Vern finally stopped long enough to ask, "Could you split a few more boxes of stove wood, Al? We're going to need that stove stoked pretty good." He showed him the chopping block and the hatchet and left a lantern swinging in the tree above him.

Tyler crooked his finger at Charlie and they went out. Tyler took down a bucket from a wooden peg, a wood bucket with a long line attached. He turned to Charlie. "Water," he said. "Brine and fresh." Not a whole sentence, but something. He pointed to the rocks beyond the house for brine and Charlie understood. There was a worn path right out to the lip of the rocks where they hung over the channel. Charlie braced himself and dropped the bucket, holding the line. It hit the water and he pulled it up, very satisfied with himself. Nothing to it. But there was no water in the bucket. As he dropped it the second time he realized that wooden buckets float, especially when they're dropped on their bottoms. So he pulled it up again and dropped it at an angle, got about a third of a bucket, and experimented until his arms were jumpy and sore from hoisting, but he had a full bucket. He brought it proudly into the cabin.

"Good," boomed Grover. " 'Bout time." he continued, and dumped the whole bucket into the black slate sink, where he was cleaning mussels.

Grover handed back the bucket to Charlie and grinned. "Need a couple more for the big fellah, there, and one at least for cleanin' the cod.

It would have been long work without Tyler. He brought buckets of fresh water up from the pump house, poured them into the cistern at the side of the sink, and began his work. He pulled a concertina out of its bag, shook it loose, and squeezed music out of it. It wailed, it sang, it chuckled, it did its own between-the-hands dance. It sang softly of foggy nights on the Banks. It rollicked around nights ashore in the taverns of Boston, London, Rio. It mourned drowned comrades. It snickered and giggled and crowed and all the while Tyler's face was soft and silent above it. It was a pleated demon he carried in a red felt bag, and it spoke all the language that Tyler didn't.

They worked to the sound of the concertina, and the sound made them a team. Charlie hoisted the buckets and his arms felt good. Al split stovewood into polite pieces. Grover cleaned and scaled a big cod, scales flying and flickering in the lantern light as Charlie waited to sluice it down with more seawater. Vern and Feynman the tailor set up a table with sawhorses and planks, benches with planks and boxes. Sarah put on an apron and worked at vegetables. At some point they began to sing.

Charlie was hoisting water and heard them start on a song he almost remembered, then

he heard his father and he knew where he had heard it. His father was singing now in a good tenor voice, dusty and slow on the beat from disuse. He hadn't sung since Charlie was small.

They take you to New Bedford,
A famous whaling port,
They give you to some land sharks
To board and fit you out, singing

Blow ye winds of the morning,
Blow ye winds heigh-ho!
Clear away your running gear
And blow, boys, blow.

And now Charlie sang, and Vern, and everyone but Feynman, who opened up the little coffin and brought out a violin. He tuned it underneath his neatly bearded chin, and started to play with Tyler: suddenly the music expanded. Not double; it expanded over and over, and Feynman's lark dived and fluttered and spun around the reedy chorus of Tyler's sparrows. They all sang, they all worked, the tiny room grew large, aroma filled it from crocks Sarah slid into the oven. The smell, the music . . . and when he was hoisting water, Charlie looked up and there were stars and the moon, and the wind!

They kept the door open, now. Charm Crawford Royal was radiating a great heat, as regal and full of personality as it had been in Charlie's dream. This was a warmth buffered by scents from the oven: bread brought rising so it was ready to glaze and bake; long-cooking parsnips; brown, round russet potatoes with butter oiling their skins; and a harmony of sweet, dessert smells that made the hinges of Charle's jaw tingle and his mouth water.

"Here he goes, this old geezer that held on so long." Grover held the big lobster, addressing it. "Well, we'll throw the shells and the leavings back in the channel, old salt, and that's what Indian Jack said his folks did to make new lobsters. And we'll apologize to you right now, and thank you for the dinner and we appreciate it. Sure do. And that's what his folks did, too, so's the rest of 'em wouldn't get cranky at our disrespect and stay out of our pots. Say goodbye, big fellah." Feynman laid a low, florid passage on the violin that must have been a funeral dirge, Sarah actually smiled at the big, blue-black impossibly designed creature, and Vern tweaked its antenna, saying "Good work, old man, for lasting this long." And into the pot he went: lid off, steam billowing, head first, lid slammed. A silence and then grisly scrapings from the boiling cauldron. "Holding still!" shouted Vern. Tyler struck up a wicked tune that Charlie didn't recognize, but Feynman knew it, took it up, and they played with demonic glee over the crustacean's misery the blasphemous American fiddle tune, "The Devil's Dream."

Sarah shook her head and went back to a platter of pickles and carrots sticks and celery ribs with their ends fuzzed.

"Can I help over here?" Al asked.

Sarah kept her eyes shyly down. "We need bread cubed for the stuffing. It's old bread, right there in the tote, and it wants to be as big as the end of your little finger, no larger." She put down her paring knife and unwrapped her parcel of tools for a longer knife. "My father gets by on what a fish knife will cut." She shook her head. "Chowders and stews."

"And what's wrong with them?" Vern was a little stung. He was lining up the plank table, about to put crockery on it.

"Nothing, occasional, like. Got to have a better meal more of the week. Take care of yourself."

"Sarah"—there was heat in his tone—"I been taking care of myself . . . and of you lot . . . for how many years?"

"Several, Pa, quite a few. Yup." Grover was invading Sarah's pile of carrot sticks.

"Get out of there, Grover. Pa, I'm not saying you ever took bad care of us or of . . . when she was still . . . all I'm saying . . ."

"I know what you're saying and I'm telling you that I feed myself and dress myself and wave bye-bye just damn fine."

"Pa—"

"I don't know, Pa," Grover interrupted, chewing another carrot stick, "but maybe she's right, like. You recall last year when you had the cold real bad after that storm and you was here alone?" At Grover's entry in the quarrel, the concertina sighed in Tyler's hands.

"No more 'o this sass, or . . ." Vern's face was red and he flexed his thick fingers.

Feynman had put down his violin and bow and was standing behind Vern with a parcel. "Mr. Filson."

"And you." Vern turned to him with a loaded finger, about to open a vast cauldron of boiling family heat, but Feynman quickly put the package into Vern's surprised hands.

"A gift," he said respectfully, "for this celebration. Good wishes and that we should all have a better New Year."

"Hear, hear!" Al broke in, feeling foolish but wanting to cast his ballot against family quarrels. What in hell did he come to Maine for? "What is it, Vern? Looks like a pair of pants. No, too thick. A tent? No, too small. A very large tie?" he went on, idiotically.

"Open it, sir." Charlie said. Charlie knew family heat. "I'd like to see what it is."

Vern looked at the boy. A little sparkle returned to his eyes, but the face remained sour. "Well, here, you open it for me."

"No, sir. I couldn't. It's your present."

Feynman nodded appreciatively.

"Hm. Open it . . . Well . . . I will open her. Thank you," he growled at Feynman.

A brown parcel, twelve by thirty and as thick as a thick book, not stiff but flexible. Vern agonized over the unwrapping, trying to save the paper. He undid the twine and the two bits of paste that held down the corners of the wrapper and laid it on the rough planks of the celebration table.

There was not much color beyond the buffs and creams of the wood in Vern's cabin, so this rectangle of celestial color was like a fanfare of trumpets for the eye. The dark royal blue of the cloth within the package glowed like a jewel. Vern unfolded it many times, puzzled, until Feynman took the other end and they pulled it out together, holding it in the air like a small sky at nautical twilight, a small sky for a small, fragile world. Feynman guided Vern with movements of his head,

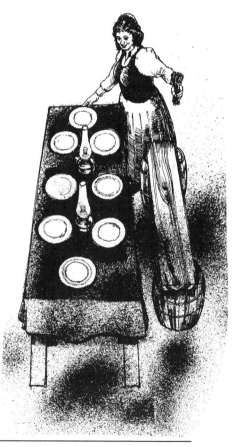

until they stood over the rough planks of the table. Sarah plucked the remaining wrapping paper from beneath it, and a brilliant tablecloth, thick and vibrant with a discreet black hem, settled into place. Al picked up the crockery and quickly laid six plates on the surfce.

"Lovely," he said, stepping back.

"Beautiful," Charlie said.

"Piss elegant," Grover opined, as Tyler squinched his eyes in embarrassment and shook his head.

Feynman turned, finally, to Vern. "That a family coming together should have a special feeling. Again, good wishes."

Vern shook his hand for the second time that evening. "Thank you, Mr. Feynman."

"Please—Nathaniel."

The table was set with plates and cups for six. Vern's worn nickelplate forks and spoons looked like charwomen dressed for the opera, surprisingly refined, and the bone-handled knives—cracked, one bound with five tight turns of copper wire—were proud and handsome as ancient veterans in a parade. Candles came out and stood at attention on the table, still unlit. Tyler put two kerosene lamps on the table, regarded them for a moment, then took them back. He found metal polish in the workshop and began to make the brass gleam. Charlie helped as well as he could, but the smells were becoming too distracting.

The lobster was done and was being dismantled by

Grover and Sarah ("Keep out o' that lobster meat, Grover!"). Vern had cleaned the mussels, steamed them, and was shucking the orange-colored meat into a bowl. The bread was almost ready; everyone could smell that. Milk on the back of the stove was heating, laying a dusty glaze of sweetness on the cabin's breath. A few potatoes were boiling for chowder, herbs were baking with the cod, making a ground scent below the other perfumes. And now, done with the lobster and with her hands washed, Sarah put a huge iron bull—cook skillet on the stove and strewed it with diced celery and onion and nut-sized pats of butter. One last smell yanked Charlie back into the kitchen, his saliva running: Feynman opened three jars of Sarah's pickles. Deep green lye pickles, long pale dill spears, and tart, sweet, burgundy-red pickled beets, as small as a baby's fist. It was too much.

"You poor thing," Sarah crooned to Charlie. He thought she would make a good mother. "You're 'bout starved, is that right? I should say you are. Here, you nibble on this . . . not you, Grover, you've had near enough for most folks' dinners. Now see if this don't keep your tummy quiet for a little while longer." She was settling something on a thick cracker, something that had a smoky smell to Charlie's sensitized nose. He bit half away and the taste was complex, musty, and good.

"What is that?" he said with his mouth full.

"Why, that's smoked herring."

"Smoked right out back here," Vern said. "These here big'ns grew up on them things as children. Muscongus Bay lollipops, yessuh."

Al was outside at the chopping stump. He felt a need for some time to sort things out. He split more of the spruce logs with Vern's axe, knocking sticks of kindling out of the barkbound rounds. It was a sharp axe with a softly curving handle. It had been a long time since he had done this work but his muscles remembered it. When he was Charlie's age over on Long's Island chopping wood was one of his chores. He could hear his grandmother calling him, telling him to work up some stovewood. As he remembered working for her he chopped harder. He picked a fleck in the wood and put the axe blace through it with just enough force to break the log with a ringing, dry *pop*. He felt a little sweaty and very satisfied. Voices from inside: he wished Tyler and Feynman would play again. He had enough kindling but he split more, then stopped and sat on the chopping stump. Laugher. A family inside. Al had a family but had never been very good at it.

Charlie came out with the bucket. "Charlie," his father called. Charlie came to him with the bucket.

There was a long silence. "Dad?"

Al nodded, but the silence went on. Finally he said, "Charlie, sometimes I think that I'm not being a very good—"

"That's not true. Don't tell me that. You're my dad. You try your best. I know that."

Laughter inside. Light breeze in the spruce over them, chilly. Charlie shivered.

"I mean, I wanted . . . but I'm not the only one who screwed up."

"Don't tell me that either. She trys, too. She's not the same as us about some things, is all. Don't tell me either of you screwed up, not tonight."

"Charlie . . ."

Charlie was cold. In town he might not have done it but here on the island it seemed okay: he put down the bucket and folded himself onto his father's lap. Al didn't try to explain anything further, just held him, remembering all the sizes of Charlie he had held, remembering far back, happy to hold him now.

As for Charlie his thoughts were more tangled. He worried about the dark side of his father's spirit but right now he loved him unquestioningly. He felt close to him in spirit, even in his father's capacity for that darkness. He was puzzled about what hung between his mother and his father, but didn't want to know, really. He wanted a home, too, a family without the strain.

They sat on the chopping stump and held each other. Charlie wondered if problems could come untangled without fussing at them. He held his strange, close, distant, skillful, clumsy dad and wished that the knots in their lives might untwist and slip smooth with nothing more than the warmth he felt from his dad. It might have been his imagination but he felt things untightening. He tightened his hug around his father's shoulders and felt the knots giving way even more.

The concertina started; a moment later the fiddle. The door opened and light poured out, then Tyler and Feynman came playing and half-dancing to the wheeling, sliding music. Sarah danced out, big and buxom and sweet-faced, holding up two lamps. Vern followed, nodding to the music and humming and carrying a big mug. Grover, carrying three mugs, began a crazy parade shuffle step. They began to sing

'Twas out of Boston we did sail,
The wind was blow-ow-ing the devil
*   of a gale,*
With our ringtail set abaft the
*   mizzen beam,*
And the dolphin striker tearing up
*   the deep,*

With a big Bow Wow,
Tow Row Row
Fol de rol de Ri Do Day.

They danced, walked, and shuffled across the clearing, singing, and as Vern passed Charlie he caught him up in his strong arm, lifted him, and pressed a big mug of cider into his hands.

The captain came from down below,
He looked aloft and he looked alow.

Grover took Al by the hand, as if to shake it, but instead lifted him to his feet and put one of the mugs in the other hand, grinning. Al took a sip of fire and sugar, Demerarra Rum and Cider. Vern took his drink from Grover and on they went, dancing, singing . . .

He looked alow and he looked aloft
Sayin' 'Coil those ropes, there, fore
*   and aft!'*
With a big Bow Wow, Tow Row
*   Row*
Fol de rol de Ri Do Day.

They danced through the spruces and out onto the rocks, dancing under the moon in the cold breeze that they did not feel, and danced back into the dark tree tunnels and past a little plot of graves with granite headstones and through granite boulders and up past the pump house, singing sea songs and mountain songs, some that Charlie knew and some he half knew, and most he had never heard—but they danced on behind the concertina and fiddle and the lights held swinging and bobbing aloft by Sarah's big, strong arms.

They danced through the last tree tunnel path, lighting it crazily as they went, Charlie watching from the middle, seeing—even though they were all happy and he was happy—a pagan parade of goblins at their ceremony.

Danced, they danced back up to the little cabin, and Al, with the rum glowing in his boilerfire now, saw a ceremony, too, and told himself. The old

man's not crazy, not much. He's dancing his defiance to the moon and the weather and the darkest night. Al began to dance higher, sing louder, addressing the darkest night of the year: Look at me, look at us. This is the low point? Think again. We're dancing, we're singing, and you've got to give us longer days from here on out. This is the worst you can do for oppression, and we aren't opressed, Jack. This for you, and he made a fine old gesture to the darkness and danced on.

The cabin was warm and the far corners dim. They stood inside the door around Sarah, still holding the lamps that lit one end of the blue, blue table. Tyler let his concertina demon sleep but Feynman went on for a time. He walked solemnly around the table playing something no one—except perhaps Sarah—had heard, something from his family's celebrations perhaps, high and frilled. Vern walked after him, lighting the candles and brass-bright lamps. The violin piece was reluctant to quit, stubbornly holding their attention because it was a blessing of a kind, curling up and looping back in flourishes on flourishes, like ornate penmanship on a treaty with fate. One last aching, clear note; the music fell and stopped.

"Best damn tailor in Bangor," Grover said to his sister.

"Welcome, everyone." Vern said.

Vern reached out to both sides of the table and took Sarah's and Feynman's hands. They reached down and took Charlie's and Tyler's hands. And they took Grover's and

Al's hands, and they joined their hands. They all looked at one another, grinned, looked at their plates or at the candles for a moment, and not even Grover spoke.

"Time to eat," Vern announced.

Sarah and Tyler got up and served mussel stew. Its surface was a beautiful white with flecks of brown potato skin, swirls of yellow butter, and crescents of orange . . . the sweet flesh of the mussels. A basket came to the table steaming through a wrapped towel: cornbread, grainy and yellow, which tasted earthy and right with the stew.

"Papa," Sarah called, and Vern got up. Charlie and Grover were clearing away the bowls from the stew, opening up a blue field in front of Vern's place.

He returned bearing a heavy plank held high and set it before them. The main course, a baked, stuffed Atlantic cod, a lowly bottom feeder, a scrabbler of dark deep places and the commonest of New England's deepwater fishes but transformed into something worthy of celebration. It had swum onto the flat board and was caught in a moment of turning. Its skin had suffered a land change, though beautifully, browned and crazed by the hot oven but retaining ragged patches of silver: brown and silver like the worn, once-gilded cover of an old manuscript. Vapor seethed around it. It sat on its frilled ruff of lobster stuffing with a dozen thin slices of lemon cut and riding its spine. Flanking the curve of its body were baked parsnips and russets. Sprigs of pine spiked the dressing and, as a joke, Grover had put a small apple in its mouth.

Quickly, the rest was placed on the table. A warm red bowl of stewed, home-canned tomatoes, a bowl of cold, tart cranberry sauce, the green pickles, a mound of pale coleslaw flecked with pepper and herbs, and a round loaf of golden crusted bread.

"It's simple enough stuff," Vern explained, "It's winter fare—what'll keep. It's how we fix it and how we eat it and how we feel doing it, makes it special. Tastes special, too." He smiled at Sarah, at Tyler and Grover. "You're good to bring it." A warm smile for Feynman, then, "Beautiful table, Nathaniel.

"And guests," he continued. "Guests who need us. Occasion for an occasion, that's what it is.

The first and best for our guests . . ." Vern cut through the cod, detached the head, and placed it respectfully on Al's plate.

"Thanks." Al said, trying hard at a pleased smile as he wondered how to eat the cod lips and goggle eyes. He would have tried it, too, if Grover hadn't broken up, guffawing. Vern giggled with him and taking back the head, replaced it with a big back filet and a spoonful of dressing, a parsnip, and a russet. Everything else followed on Al's plate, then Charlie's, then the rest.

"Sakes!" Tyler cried and rose quickly. He went out the door and was gone for a couple of minutes. He came back in with a damp case of beer, probably

forgotten in the dinghy. The beer bottles had strange tops, porcelain plugs with rubber washers and wire closures.

"Hell, yes," Vern called as soon as he saw the beer. "Cups!"

Charlie smelled the malty tang of the beer as it foamed to the rim of the mugs all around him. His father liked beer. Sarah poured more cider for Charlie.

"To our hosts." Al raised his glass, "New friends, good food. To families." He drank off a third of his beer.

"Mazel tov," Feynman said, and took a sip.

"Families," Sarah said, blushing.

Grover said, "Fair winds." Tyler added in a small voice, "And following seas."

Vern smiled. "Families." He drank down most of his glass and giggled again.

The cod had a clean taste, big moist white flakes eaten with the rich buttery lobster dressing. Beer bottles began to make an impressive row against the wall. The buttered russet potatoes, always tasting a little like the earth, and the sweet parsnips agreed with each other. Charlie liked eating them with canned tomatoes and the puckery-sweet cranberry sauce. The wonderful smells stayed alive in the air. They kept eating hungrily until the cod was picked clean and the dressing was done and Charlie ate the last pickle

"Whew," Vern said. "Eat like that every day, it'd kill us. Where's dessert?"

Sarah made a clatter at the counter for three or four minutes while Grover and Tyler and Charlie cleaned off the table and stacked the plates, the silver, the bowls. By unspoken agreement the boys left all the cups on the table with the family heads—Vern and Al and Nathaniel—and the line of beer bottles grew.

Al turned to Nathaniel. "Business in Bangor goes well?" he asked, examining the structure of the bubbles in his beer.

"Well. Very well, getting better each month. People know quality."

"Do you use a computer for your patterns?"

"Oh, yes. I compute the yardage, the stretch, the fit with tables. Perhaps big companies have a man who computes everything; for us—myself and three tailors working for me—I compute. The key is quality. Customer goes away with a piece of goods on his back, likes it, likes the way it hangs, you see, the way it wears. Says, I look good in this piece of goods I got at Feynman the Tailor's. Hey, Mo, he says to his brother"—Feynman poured himself more beer—"your vest, your pants. They don't look too good, not like mine. Need new. Go to—"

"Feynman the Tailor: Quality Counts, Customers Confirm!" Al broke in with his best announcer's voice.

"Good!" Feynman said, "That's good. A good . . . what is it?"

"Slogan."

"It's very good. I'll ask Herschel and Martin and Richard what they think."

Vern put his cup down and looked into it. He spoke deliberately, putting his words in individual pieces of time so they would be the ones he wanted. "I am glad that your business is going well. You are good to come."

Feynman spoke to him in his own formal way, drawing himself up. "Sarah is as good a wife as a man could have. I know your own wife passed away. She should rest in peace. I have to thank just you for my happiness. For me, I try to be a husband like a loving father would want. We, you and I, are not of the same faith; we are, though, of the same honor. I prize Sarah like jewels, like . . ." Feyn-

man struggled to shape the right phrase with his hands in the air. The beer had opened him up, and the man inside was full of flourish, like his music.

"Yup. Yup, I see that. You are good to come. She was a good daughter. She's a good girl." He looked toward Sarah working at the counter, blushing. "A good wife to you."

"She is still a good daughter." Feynman corrected him respectfully but firmly. Vern did not reply but kept looking at Sarah, solid and still graceful, spooning whipped cream.

Vern turned back and smiled, then Feynman, then Al.

"Dessert." Sarah announced. On the table she sat a lattice-crust blueberry pie made with her own canned blueberries and a whole-wheat crust. She returned in a moment with a crumb-crust apple pie and a wedge of white cheddar on a square of maple plank. A deep pot of Indian pudding came next, its surface steaming sullenly, dark with deep orange lights like the face of a tarnished cymbal. Finally, as Charlie brought plates and washed bowls, she set a cold bowl of whipped cream, smelling of vanilla, in the center.

"I can't decide." Charlie worried.

"Then take your time," Grover advised, "Little bit o' this, little bit o' that. Try it all."

"Good plan," Al agreed.

The Indian pudding was probably the best, but the apple pie and cheese went together so well, although the blueberry pie with whipped cream was splendid. He tried them all again. Results were inconclusive. No one could decide and finally everyone had all three on their plates.

Charm Crawford Royal, the stove, was heating water for tea and coffee and dishwashing. The first sinkful of washing was going along with Sarah, who insisted, and Grover, who surprised everybody. Tyler was beginning to finger the buttons on his concertina and Feynman eyed his violin case. Charlie was sitting with his father when Vern caught his eye.

"Your Charlie has got somethin' for you. Don't ya, Charlie." Charlie slipped off the bed they were sitting on and went

around the table to the shop. He returned with something held behind his back.

"Al, this is the darkest time of the year and we give each other little pieces of hope, little presents that say things aren't that bad, hold out, spring's comin'. Charlie?"

"I made this. Mr. Filson showed me how but I made it. It's for your boots." and he handed the bootjack to his father.

"Charlie. A bootjack. I am just . . . Charlie, it's something, it's really a piece of work. You did this whole thing? It's beautiful. Tremendous. Charlie, it makes me really happy." Yet it seemed to give him more pain than pleasure.

"You don't like it?"

"Aw, Charlie, I love it. I'm so damn touched. I'm kind of upset because I don't have anything for you."

Vern waved one big, stained hand, "Sure you do. You just don't know it, is all."

Al thought a moment. Thinking seemed easy, here even with all the beer. Things seemed clear. Maybe there was a part of himself he could give the boy.

"Take it easy, Al," Vern said. "Things will come along. Right now"—Vern got to his feet, not entirely steady—"you better get used to acceptin' things graceful. Got something in here for you. Best kind of thing for a man as puts stock in engines." He reached up above the door of the shop and swung down and into the cabin a pair of spruce oars, shaped in planes like the long bones of a wading bird, yellow from linseed oil, brown leather tacked around the shaft where they would meet the rowlocks, graceful, light. "Filson oars," Vern said proudly. "And may you have luck with 'em."

Grover nodded in agreement with Al's look. "Yup, fine as kind. This old man makes as good a pair of looms as you'll find on the coast. That's a fact. Hell, you'll throw that 'ere engine away, you use them oars a spell. Nice pair, Pa."

Vern beamed.

"Vern, I . . . "

"Al, just you have another drink here and let me thank you again. You've given me more than you know. Me and the boys and"—he looked over his shoulder to where she was washing dishes with Grover— "and my Sarah. Mr. Feynman . . . Nathaniel, too. Sometimes, just being there, a person can make a difference in hope. You gave us a lot on the darkest day, Al. You, too, Charlie."

"Thank you, Mr. Filson. I'm having a wonderful time."

"A wonderful time! Hear that, Tyler? Nathaniel? Whip us up a new tune!"

They played. Loud and long and even more like goblins with pleasant faces, their elbows jumping to the bow and the squeezing. The dishes were done and Sarah danced with her father and with Grover, a jig or hornpipe or whatever it was. The beer bottle line grew longer, the music crept into their ears and filled up their heads, and they could feel it with their feet and their shoulders and their hair. The cabin glowed orange and white and brass, brighter with the music. Al noticed that the boy was asleep beside him, his head, his dear head that Al loved, in his lap. Al wondered how he could sleep on a night like this, with this music and these people. Al grinned at Vern and Grover and they grinned back at him, the music painting the air between them, and a minute later Al was asleep, too, the music still in his head but very far away.

The music was finished but still in their heads. They woke together just after sunrise, Charlie and his father. They were alone in the cabin, which had been tidied around them. The beer bottles were collected (Al wondered why he felt so fine after so many beers), the plank table had been dismantled, and the planks wrestled back into the shop. The blue tablecloth lay folded on the counter. The floor was swept, everything in the little cabin was neat and clean.

On the table near the window were two plates with wedges of apple pie and cheese and two forks. A jug of cider sat beside them. Breakfast.

They came out into the morning. The split wood in the woodyard had been tidied. The whole cabin was so neat it looked as if it were ready to be packed away in cottonwool, just so. Al went back inside and fetched his oars. They were light and easy to carry down to the boat. But all this time they had not seen Vern or Grover or Tyler or Sarah or Feynman . . . where were they? Vern or Sarah had left breakfast for them. They were fishermen though, accustomed to early hours; they would tend their pots and retun in the late afternoon. "We'll come back tomorrow," Al replied to Charlie's questioning glance, "and bring some presents of our own." Charlie smiled.

Charlie got into the boat; Al coiled the long line and pushed off. The garvey floated free. The oar-locks dangled from

their sockets. Al fitted them into place and the oars slipped into them. He held the handles and felt the slight weight of the Filson oars over the water. He did not dip them in, yet.

"Charlie," he began, "did I ever tell you what my family was like when I was a little kid?"

"No. You never talked about it."

"Well . . . " he dipped the oars and pulled, the Whaler responding to the slight flex of the beautiful oars. "Things were kind of angry around our place. We never did much together. I was lonely and scared a part of the time. One Christmas . . . " Al continued to work the oars, bend, dip, pull, recover, and to open himself to Charlie about his own crippled family and why he had wanted a family all his life. It was a strange gift, difficult to give. The rowing helped; gliding over the morning calm, the quickened breathing and the strained speech that go with rowing covered up some of the emotion of opening up. They covered a good part of the passage that way. Charlie asked some questions that Al wanted to answer and some that Al couldn't answer right away. He asked for some time to think about those. As for the rest of the passage, they sang. Some were raucous songs, some they could sing softly, some they had learned the night before.

Al was remembering how to row. He looked behind him to check his direction and then looked quickly to a spot behind Charlie's head. As long as he kept that spot stationary on Charlie's ear they were going straight, except when a cross-current crabbed them sideways. For long periods Al would row to these marks, and he was doing well when they came up to the landing dock at Cletus Marine. Charlie was singing with Al, a low, slow song, when he looked up.

Spanish is the lovin' tongue
Sweet as music, soft as rain . . .,

Al sang on, though Charlie had stopped.

"Hello, sailor." Her voice, his wife's, Charlie's mother, his enemy, his love. What she had to say wasn't in the words she spoke. There were paragraphs

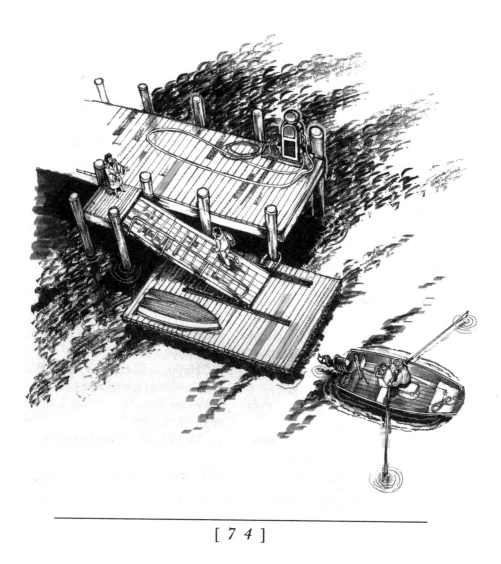

of meaning in her tone: the low register, the sadness, the anxiety of her phrasing. He had known her almost all of his adult life and knew everything she had to tell him in those two words. All the surrender, some of the holdout defiance, most of all the care. What it must have cost her to come here! Still he could not believe her, refused for a moment to look back, and drifted with the Filson oars held parallel to the dark water's surface.

He dipped one oar moving into the water so that the boat's drift turned him toward the dock. His eyes fell on her and held steady as the boat turned.

She looked at him, pleading.

He looked back, uncertain.

Al pushed at the oars and backed the boat into the dinghy float. When the garvey touched the float Charlie leaped out to run up the gangway. His leap pushed the boat outward.

Charlie threw his arms around his mother. Being close to his father, closer than ever, had made him thirsty for being close to her. He smelled her and felt her familiar in his hug. He was so glad she was here.

Al watched from the boat. He tried out the oars a little longer, confused as to what he should, or could, say. The oars were beautiful. Vern's present. Vern's family. Al had seen something underneath the gaiety, something for the time when there was not a crowd of people on Marsh Island: Vern's loneliness.

She spoke to Al again. "I

missed you." Charlie, holding her, heard her voice, large and a trifle unsteady, through the ear pressed to her shoulder.

Charlie saw his father nod, yes. His mouth opened and closed once but he did not speak, yet.

Al spun the boat: forward on the starboard oar, aft on the port. Good oars.

"I worried," she said. It wasn't accusing; it was confessional.

He nodded. Stopped the boat. Cleared his throat. Twice. "Beth." He stopped for a moment, savoring her name in his mouth. "I'm sorry. Really." He could not take his eyes away from her, now. She was a pretty woman, and he knew her so well. He wanted to let his old

anger go. What if he thought of his anger and sadness as part of another year? Part of the year before the solstice, anger gone by and the world coming into more light? He gave a few pulls on the oars and drifted away from the dinghy float. He tried to remember what Feynman had said, very late, about his own family's New Year: there was a time of atonement, when you put the sins, the angers, the hurts of the old year to rest. Al saw her face even out here, the face he wanted to see. The worry and the sorrow were on it, enough to atone for any of his sorrows. "Hey," he called.

Charlie watched his father dance with the oars and the boat, swinging it inshore and offshore with a soft hiss and rustle of water on spruce and fiberglass. It was a slow, graceful dance, and his father's face was beautiful, his father's hands were skillful, his father's voice was warm. "Hey," his father called.

"Al?" she replied.

"I love you."

She smiled and nodded, me too.

Charlie held his mother and held his father in his eyes and felt clumps of knots give away. Knots, there would always be knots, but the tangle had become less hurtful.

Mr. Cletus from the boatyard was coming out to the dock. "There you are. Lady here worried sick about you two fellahs. Good work that you're safe and sound. What in the world happened to you out there?"

"Engine conked out," Charlie said.

"Out in the channel below Marsh Island," Al said. "We drifted up the channel and saw a light, managed to paddle in with a cooler top and a seat cushion."

"Those look a sight better than cooler tops," Cletus said.

"These. You bet. A fellow out on Marsh Island took us in for the night. His family showed up. Beth, it was the best night. You've got to meet him."

"Mom, it was so cool. He had two sons and a daughter he hadn't—

Cletus shook his head, "No one out on Marsh Island this season."

"Well, there sure is. He made these oars. He and his family were out there. Two boys, Grover and Tyler. Had sailboats, lobstermen. They came last night."

"No lobstermen fishing off no sailboats, neither. Don't mean to contradict. Just none of 'em do it."

"Someone better tell whoever makes the winter census that there is somebody out there. Hell, what if Vern got in trouble, or something?"

"Okay. Anyway, glad you're safe, glad for the lady here. You want to leave that engine, we'll get to it in the spring. I'll be in the shed. Glad to see you." And he started away. He turned back. "Tell you this. Anyone'd know about that island and people on it, it'd be Stanton Frederick there." He pointed down the shore. A hundred yards away, crowded by spruces, sat an imposing green-shingled house with tiers of porches and a windowed cupola at its crown.

"Yes?" Stanton Frederick looked liked a retired professor. He was eighty or thereabouts, and had dark, age-tanned skin. The fringe about his bald pate seemed shockingly white.

Al raised the oars upright and rested their butt ends on the porch floor. "Hello, I'm Al Ives from Boston, Massachusetts. This is my wife and my boy. We've been coming up to my uncle's cabin for some years—"

"Yes, I know him well. We raced together. In the thirties."

"That would be him, yes. Mr. Cletus and I disagree on a small matter and we thought you might be of help."

"I know little about mechanics."

"No, not that. My boy and I were . . . well, it's a long story and it boils down to this—do you know Vern Filson?"

"Vern? Oh, yes, what a character. What a seaman. And a craftsman—Vern Filson and his oars and his pots. Yes, I know Vern Filson."

Al turned to Beth and smiled.

"Yes, I knew him right up into the thirties."

"He's not that old, is he?"

"No, he's not. He's dead."

Charlie looked up at Frederick, then at his father. They looked at each other in confusion.

"Yes, died in the early forties. Died alone, a troubled man. His little place out on Marsh burned down one night about this time of the year. Stove or chimney fire or something. Troubled man but enormously—are you well?"

Al did not speak at first. "Perhaps," he said in a cautious voice, "someone is living in his house."

"Oh, I think not. No. Come with me. I'll show you something you seldom see. Up this way, follow me. It's quite a few landings, I fear, and I stop on every one. There, see? First one. Getting old. There. Come summer this big drafty place will be full of relatives, children. Whew. Third landing, two to go. You, young man, when you get over whatever fright you seem to have had, you come over and see me, then, and meet the tribe. Lord, there are a lot of them.

"Here we are." They had come all the way up into the cupola at the steep peak of the roof. "Have you ever seen one of these? It's the spotting binocular from a Japanese destroyer. Monstrous, isn't it? I was on a Navy destroyer during the war, you see, and this was given to me. Reparations." He chuckled briefly, a sound as thin as an icepick, "Now let me see." He swung the haybale-sized gray-metal binoculars this way and that, tilting them slightly up, stronger than he seemed. He rotated the focus knob above. It was obvious that he spent time with the huge glasses. "Yes, yes, a little more . . . there. Take a look, young man. That is Vern Filson's cabin."

Charlie sat on the stool behind the eyepieces and looked apprehensively into the deep glass lenses. His eyes adjusted. The cove, the spruces, and there, the charred ruin reaching out over the rocks, the weeds growing up through the ruin.

Al looked. Beth looked. The old man smiled and put the dust covers over the lenses.

They walked down two flights to the study behind the

old man. They didn't say a word. Al and Charlie were silenced by shock. She was quiet for them.

"Filson was a character, but he was a craftsman. Those oars. Look at these." Frederick took a pair of oars browned with age from a rack in the corner. The old man held them up beside the new oars Al had left on the landing. "They're a set of brothers. Look at that," he marveled, "the same planes, the same proportions, the same shapes. Who made these? They're beautiful."

Al looked at him with weary resignation. "Vern Filson made these oars for me last night. There's his mark: *V.F.* He took us in when we were drenched and warmed us in his cabin, which was not burnt down, and fed us, and we danced around the island because of the solstice."

There was a shift in Frederick's face.

"Vern saved us. That's all I know."

Frederick touched Al's oars with the tip of one thin finger. There was a look of intelligent anger that his age could never soften. "The oil is still wet, Mr. Ives." He held his index finger up from the sharp curve where the oar handles made into the shaft. The anger deepened and he said coldly, "Please leave my house."

Al nodded, accepting Frederick's anger as his share of the blame for being a dreamer. "Excuse me. We . . . I had no wish to offend you, Mr. Frederick. It's merely what happened. It's what we saw. But I understand."

Outside, Al started down the porch stairs alone, but she caught up and put her hand in his. Charlie took his other hand. "Mr. Ives," Frederick called down to him from the study window. "Just a moment."

The front door opened and Frederick beckoned to Al. Charlie and his mother followed. He looked at them a little suspiciously.

"It's all right," Al said. "They can hear whatever you have to say."

"I'm old, Mr. Ives. I'm older than I planned to be. I don't sleep well anymore. When I knew Filson I was young and he was full of opinions. One, about the solstice, always sticks in my mind. Maybe I even agree with him, for once.

"I couldn't sleep last night and I took a drink of sherry. I walked around the house and fetched up in the cupola." Frederick looked around him as if unseen others were trying to hear a crazy old man. "I looked out there, late. I saw something, I think. Out on the rocks, then into the woods, around the island, lights bobbing. Maybe I saw . . . something else. I don't think so."

"What?"

"Mr. Ives, there are things that rational men do not believe, no matter what arguments or how persistent. Perhaps you are not frightened. But I am closer to my reckoning. I am. Those are Filson oars. It may be that by summer I shall no longer be here. If I am, we can discuss it. Not now. Enough for today. Enough. Forgive my rudeness. Madam, young man. Good day."

"One more thing."

"No."

"Do you know Bangor well?" The white hair nodded, well enough. "In Bangor, is there a Feynman, a tailor?"

"Yes. In a brick building near the depot. Written on the side of the building for years, even after he was gone . . ."

"Gone?"

"His wife died in childbirth. Feynman simply left town, nobody knew where. He was grief-stricken, they say. Yes, the sign was there for years, faded, until the building was torn down: *Feynman the Tailor: Quality Counts, Customers Confirm.*"

"Sarah Filson was Feynman's wife."

"I wouldn't know. Vern's daughter ran off to Bangor, and he never spoke her name again."

"His boys?"

"Drowned, both of them in the same storm. Lobstering is a dangerous profession. We recovered their remains up-bay and buried them on Marsh Island."

"In a little plot up from the rocks?"

"Enough."

"We danced around it twice."

"You must leave. I'm sorry.

You must go." The old man turned back into the house and shut the door against them. They heard his voice once more. "Enough sadness for one year."

They sat in the car, unwilling to turn on the engine. Beth said, "I know you, Al. You've done some crazy things but you're not crazy. I do trust you. Don't start to think I don't. You're not crazy. Don't start to think it. I don't. I love you, Al."

He nodded.

Charlie put his hand on his father's shoulders from the back seat. "Maybe you're crazy, Dad, but I'm not, and I saw the same things, ate the same Indian pudding. You're okay, Dad." His father's shoulders felt strong.

His mother leaned across and put her forehead on Al's shoulder for a second. "Yup."

He started the engine.

"Dad?"

"What, Charlie?"

"Should we go back? Next solstice?"

A long silence, the car's engine idling. Al's head shook slowly. No, not ever.

"Wait! The bootjack. It's in the garvey's box." Charlie jumped out the back door and ran down to the trailer at the landing. He climbed in and pulled it out of the center seat box. It was a nice piece of oak. Charlie was proud of it. He looked across the water to the Marsh Island headland: there, where the cove would be—a dark smudge at this distance— he saw something. What might be a wisp of smoke, the smoke that might come from splits of spruce in a Charm Crawford Royal, just a wisp.

His father blew the horn once. Charlie climbed down and walked backward up the ramp. Then he turned and ran to the car. It was time to go home.